To Adam
S. M^CB.

For Di
A. J.

Text copyright © 2007 by Sam McBratney
Illustrations copyright © 2007 by Anita Jeram

Guess How Much I Love You™ is a registered trademark
of Walker Books Ltd., London.

First U.S. edition 2008
First Midi Hardcover edition 2009
This edition published specially for Book of the Month Club,
2009 by Candlewick Press

Library of Congress Cataloging-in-Publication Data is available.
Library of Congress Catalog Card Number 2007927626

ISBN 978-0-7636-3546-6
(Candlewick Case-bound BB edition)
ISBN 978-0-7636-4904-3
(BOMC Midi Hardcover edition)

09 10 11 12 SCP 10 9 8 7 6 5 4 3 2 1

Printed in Humen, Dongguan, China

This book was typeset in Cochin.
The illustrations were done in
ink and watercolor.

Candlewick Press
99 Dover Street
Somerville, Massachusetts 02144

visit us at www.candlewick.com

WHEN I'M
BIG

by
Sam McBratney

illustrated by
Anita Jeram

CANDLEWICK PRESS

Little Nutbrown Hare
and Big Nutbrown Hare went
hopping in the fresh spring air.

Spring is when things start
growing after winter.

They saw a tiny acorn growing.

"Someday it will be a tree,"
said Big Nutbrown Hare.

"A big, big tree?"

"Oh, a mighty tree,"
said Big Nutbrown
Hare.

Little Nutbrown Hare spotted a tadpole
in a pool. It was a tiny tadpole,
as wriggly as
could be.

"It will grow up to be a frog,"
said Big Nutbrown Hare.

"Like that frog over there?"

"Just the same as that one,"
said Big Nutbrown Hare.

A hairy caterpillar slowly crossed the
path in front of them, in search of
something green to eat.

"One day soon it will change
into a butterfly," said
Big Nutbrown Hare.

"With wings?"

"Oh, lovely wings," said
Big Nutbrown Hare.

And then they found a bird's nest
among the rushes. It was full of eggs.

"What does an egg turn into?" asked
Little Nutbrown Hare.

"A bird."

"A big, big bird?"

"Well . . . a grown-up bird,"
said Big Nutbrown Hare.

Does nothing stay the same? thought Little Nutbrown Hare. Does everything change?

Then he began to laugh.

"What does a little
brown hare like
me turn into?"
he asked.

Big Nutbrown Hare
begain to think,

and think. . . .

Goodness me, did he
know the answer?

Yes, he did!

"You'll be a Big Nutbrown Hare—like me!"